Jane Hissey

Ruff

SCRIBBLERS

O LD Bear, Bramwell Brown and Little Bear were listening at the door. 'I can hear a "ruff, ruff" noise outside,' said Old Bear. 'Let's see what it is.'

HE opened the door and something woolly bounced in!

'Who are you?' gasped Old Bear.

'I'm a dog,' said their visitor.

'We can see that,' said Little Bear.

'But what's your name?'

'I'VE never had a name,' said the dog.

'Shall we call you Ruff?' suggested Little Bear. 'Because that's the noise you make.'

'I love that name,' said Ruff.

'WHERE have you come from?' asked Duck.

'I was left in the garden,' said Ruff. 'Nobody seems to want me.'

'Perhaps you were a bit bouncy,' said Little Bear.

'Everyone's bouncy when they are young,' said Bramwell kindly.

'How old are you, Ruff?'

UFF counted his paws.

'**One, two, three, four...**' then he added his ears,

'**...five, six...**' and his nose,

'**...seven!**' he said. 'I think I'm seven.'

'Don't you know?' gasped Little Bear.

'I always count my birthdays.'

'I've never had a birthday,' said Ruff.

'IF you stay,' said Bramwell, 'we could give you a birthday tomorrow.'

'We could give Ruff seven birthdays!' said Old Bear. 'One for every year he's missed!'

'An all-week birthday!' said Rabbit. 'Whoopee!'

MONDAY was Ruff's first birthday.

'Happy birthday, Ruff,' cried the toys. They all gave him presents: a rubber bone, a new collar, two pairs of boots and three balls. Bramwell made him a special cake with a candle on it.

'It smells lovely,' said Ruff. But some of the icing stuck to his nose.

'Ah-tish-ooo!' He sneezed out his candle and everyone sang 'Happy Birthday to Ruff!'

T UESDAY was Ruff's second birthday.

'Let's play treasure hunts,' said Little Bear and he hid all Ruff's presents.

The toys had great fun looking for them. They found everything except one green ball. It was down Little Bear's trousers!

'I thought they were a bit lumpy!' he said.

Ruff's cake had two candles this time. He blew them out very carefully.

W EDNESDAY was Ruff's third birthday.

His new friends had made him cards. Ruff read them again and again – the right way up, upside down, inside out and back to front.

'Look at your jelly cake,' said Little Bear. 'It has three candles.'

Ruff took a deep breath.

'*Phooooooo!*'

Out went the candles and down went the cards.

'What a lot of cards,' said Ruff happily. 'That's how many friends I have.'

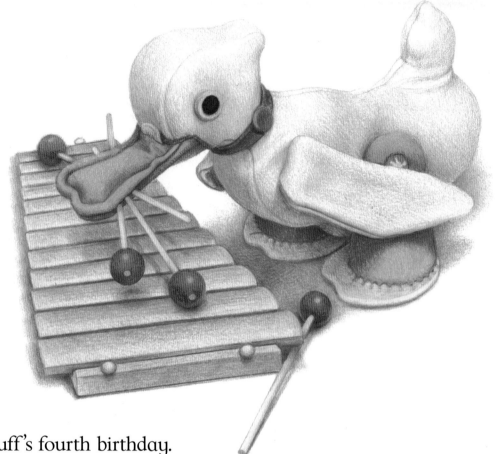

T HURSDAY was Ruff's fourth birthday.

'Time for musical chairs,' said Old Bear.

Duck played the music and, when he stopped, the toys all sat on a cushion.
Ruff sat on Rabbit by mistake.

'I think you are out!' said Little Bear. But they let him stay in the game
because it was his birthday.

Ruff only had enough puff to blow out three candles, but he wagged his tail
so hard the last one went out too!

FRIDAY was Ruff's fifth birthday. Old Bear wrapped up
a huge, lumpy package.

'We are going to play pass the parcel,' he said.

The toys sat in a circle and passed the parcel round and round. When the
music stopped, the person holding the parcel took off one piece of paper.

But Ruff was so excited he tore off all the paper to find the prize.

'THAT'S not the way to play,' said Old Bear. Ruff was very sorry and let everyone play with his prize and blow out the candles on his cake.

SATURDAY was Ruff's sixth birthday.

'Today we'll have a birthday treat,' said Bramwell Brown. The toys had made a train out of cardboard boxes.

'You can be the train driver,' they told Ruff.

'All aboard!' he cried.

He was in such a hurry, he nearly set off without Little Bear!

W HEN the train stopped, Ruff counted the candles on his cake.

'One, two, three, four, five, six... oh dear,' he sighed. 'Tomorrow will be my last birthday.'

'Not really,' said Old Bear. 'After that you will have one birthday every year, just like the rest of us.'

SUNDAY was Ruff's seventh birthday, but when he woke up there was nobody there.

'They've forgotten about me,' thought Ruff. 'It must be time to go.'

He wrote a note saying, 'Thank you for a lovely time, love Ruff.'

Then he picked up his bundle of presents. But when he opened the door... there were all his friends!

'HAPPY birthday, Ruff!' they cried, and they gave him a lovely cushion decorated with all his favourite things.

'We want you to stay with us,' said Little Bear. 'And this is your very own place to sleep.' Ruff jumped straight onto his cushion.

'That is just what I've always wanted,' he sighed. 'Thank you!'
And they all agreed Ruff's seventh birthday was the happiest one of all.

For James and Elizabeth

SALARIYA

www.salariya.com

This edition published in Great Britain in MMXIII by Scribblers, a division of Book House,
an imprint of The Salariya Book Company Ltd
25 Marlborough Place,
Brighton BN1 1UB

www.scribblersbooks.com
www.janehissey.co.uk

First published in Great Britain in MCMXCIV by Hutchinson Children's Books

ISBN-13: 978-1-908973-18-4

3 5 7 9 8 6 4 2

A CIP catalogue record for this book is available from the British Library.

Printed and bound in China
Printed on paper from sustainable sources
Reprinted in MMXIII